little.com

To Andy's mum, Jean –
and Terry, his dad

little.com

Ralph STEADman

Andersen Press

London

First published in Great Britain in 2000 by Andersen Press Ltd.,
20 Vauxhall Bridge Road, London SW1V 2SA.
Published in Australia by Random House Australia Pty.,
20 Alfred Street, Milsons Point, Sydney, NSW 2061.
All rights reserved.
Colour separated in Switzerland by Photolitho AG, Zürich.
Printed and bound in Italy by Grafiche AZ and Legapress, Verona.

10   9   8   7   6   5   4   3   2   1

British Library Cataloguing in Publication Data available.

ISBN 0 86264 994 3

The illustrations are acrylic, gouache and Indian ink on
white cartridge, torn and recrafted on CM 100/100
cotton Fabriano. This book has been printed on acid-free paper.

This work is available in a special edition of which
300 copies are numbered and signed by the artist,
cloth bound and presented in a slip case.
ISBN 0 86264 984 6

I am a dot. I live inside your computer, so you will always know where to find me. What nobody knows is that I have a secret. So please don't tell anyone.

My secret is this . . .

. . . Every time you switch off, I sneak away to have tea with my friend the Duchess of Amalfi.

She lives in a castle on a hill.

I whizz through space to her place.

Zip,
zap,
zoom,
and I'm there!

But before I set out for the castle I like to dress up.

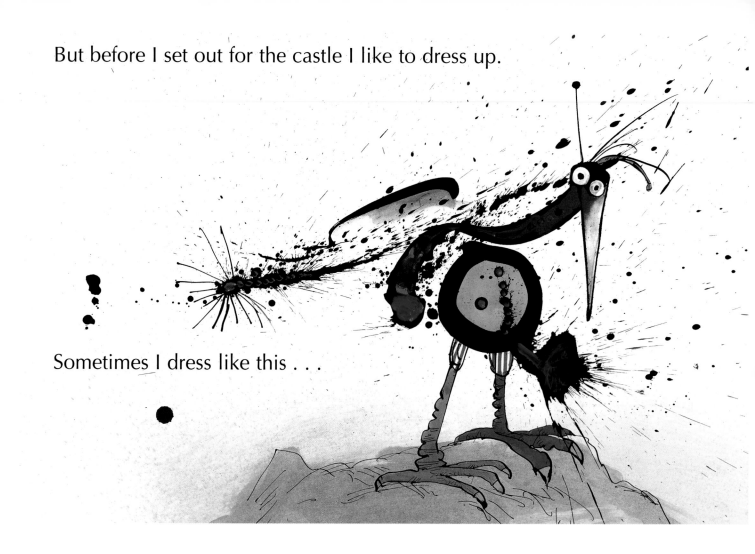

Sometimes I dress like this . . .

. . . and sometimes I dress like this.

The Duchess knows I don't like tea. She gives me INK.
I LOVE INK!

When I am full of ink
I feel wobbly . . .

. . . and wacky.

Once I have had my ink with the Duchess, I roll down the hill and scare the awful Duke of Bogshott and his White Army. He is always hanging about because he wants to live in the Duchess's castle.

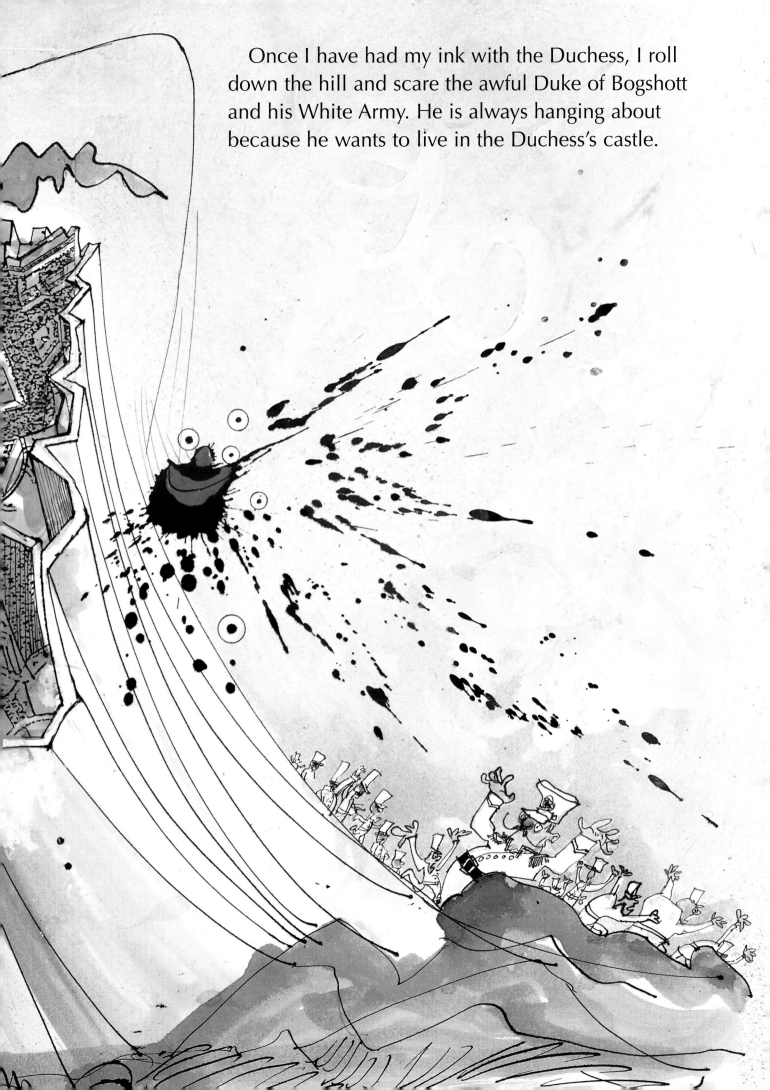

When the Duke's White Army sees me sploshing ink everywhere, they run away.

"LOOK OUT!" they shout, and leap for cover.

I splatter the slowest soldiers all over their backs. I wet their socks, too. There is nothing soldiers hate more than marching about in inky, wet socks.

I make a real racket.
The Duke puts a finger to his mouth
and whispers, "Sshhsshhsshh!
You'll wake the enemy."

"I haven't got any enemies!"
I shout. "EVERYBODY LOVES ME!"

I pretend to be a tiger and roar very loudly.
The Duke of Bogshott pretends not to be frightened,
and stands to attention.

I cover him in ink from head to foot.

Then I feel ashamed of myself, so I dance for the soldiers. And they dance, too.

I'm pretty good, and so long as I don't wiggle I hardly make a single blot.

But sometimes I get carried away . . .

...YIPPEE!

Last Thursday I tried to fly down the hill after visiting the
Duchess, but I was so full of ink that I crash-landed.
When I stood up I looked a proper mess. And so did the Army!

On Sunday, the Duchess gave me a real surprise – a pair of roller blades! I whizzed back down the hill like a mad thing.

Today another unexpected thing happened. I went to visit the Duchess as usual and the Duke of Bogshott was waving a white flag of surrender. It was covered in blots.

"Please," he said, "will you take me to meet the Duchess? You always seem to have such a good time."

Sometimes you have to trust people just as much as dots. So I let him follow me up the hill. The Duke and Duchess fell in love at once. But that made me worried. Would I be invited again? The Duchess read my thoughts. "Don't be upset, little dot. We are getting married next Tuesday. You can be our BEST MAN."

I was so excited I made a mess on her carpet.

Then I said, "But I am not a man. I am a DOT!"
"Well then," said the Duchess, "you can be our
BEST DOT – the BEST DOT in the whole world!"
I did a somersault right there on the spot –
and a little dot on the ceiling.

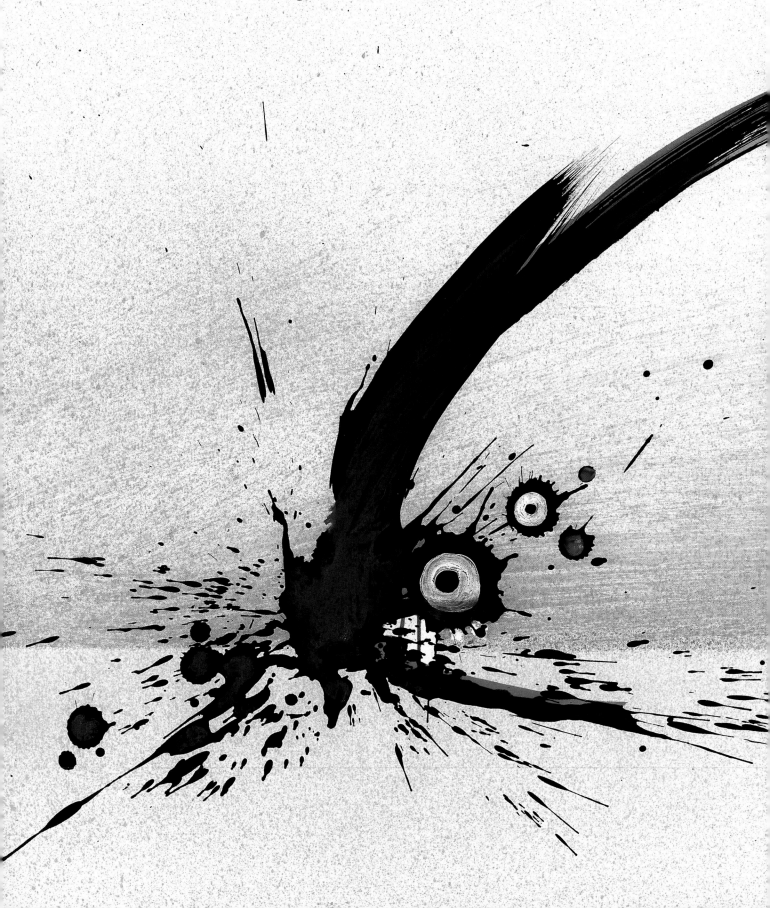

"WHOOPEE!" I screamed. "I will dress up as the best Best Dot ever. I will wear a whole sockful of RED ink. RED is so smart for a wedding."

"Then I," said the Duchess, "shall wear BLACK, and you can splash about as much as you like."

When the Duke heard this he blushed with happiness. He went as red as my sock! He asked his bride if she would wear the regimental, barbed-wire wedding dress which had belonged to his mother.

And the Duchess agreed!

WHAT a good job I rushed back when I did, because you had just switched on your computer. And here I am, ready to work for you again – dot dot dot

But remember, please do NOT tell anyone
our secret or someone will stop me
going out ever again . . .

. . . and you know where
I have to be next Tuesday

dot

dot

dot

dot

DOT !